Just Enough and Not Too Much

— BY KAETHE ZEMACH —

ARTHUR A. LEVINE BOOKS
An Imprint of Scholastic Inc.

This
PJ BOOK
belongs to

_____

_____

PJ Library
JEWISH BEDTIME STORIES and SONGS

IN LOVING MEMORY OF MY PARENTS

—K. Z.

SIMON THE FIDDLER had a
cozy little house and everything he needed.

He had a chair to sit on,

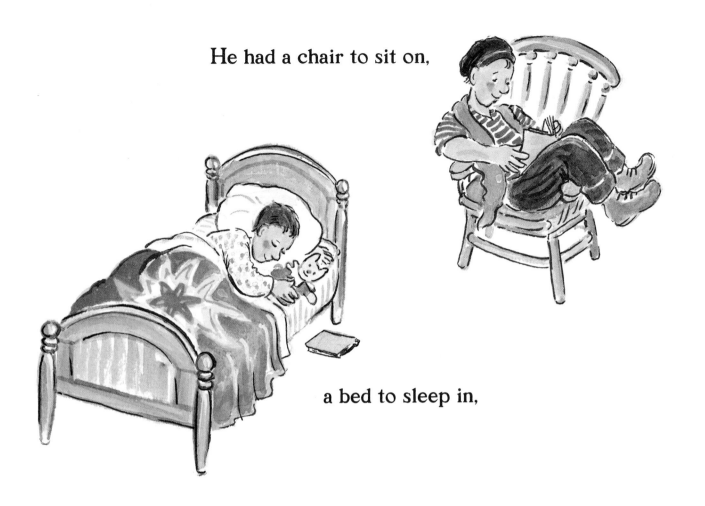

a bed to sleep in,

food to eat,

clothes to wear,

a soft hat,

a toy animal,

good friends,

and a beautiful fiddle,
with a voice as sweet as honey.

For a long time, Simon was perfectly happy.
He took care of his house, spent time with his friends,
and played the fiddle to his heart's content.

But one day, Simon looked around his little house
and thought, "I don't have enough."

I WANT MORE!

So, Simon got another chair.

And another,

and another,

and then a few more.

Soon, Simon had many chairs!

But still, Simon thought, "I don't have enough."
So, he got another hat.

And another,

and another,

and then a few more.

Soon, Simon had many hats!

But still, Simon thought, "I don't have enough."
So, he got another toy animal.

And another,

and another,

and then a few more.

Soon, Simon had many toy animals.

And for a while, he enjoyed having MORE!

Until Simon noticed that
his house was getting crowded.

In fact, it got so crowded, he could hardly move around!

Simon missed his simple life. He missed taking care of his house,
spending time with his friends, and playing his beautiful fiddle.
"I have TOO MUCH!" Simon cried.

So, he set up a long table and put his chairs around it.
Then, he put a hat and a toy animal on the table
in front of each chair.

Simon decorated his house, baked a cake,
and when everything was ready, invited his friends
to come to a wonderful party.

When Simon's friends arrived, they said,
"Hello! It's been so long!" Then they sat on the chairs,
put on the hats, and played with the many toy animals.

And it was indeed a wonderful party!
Everyone talked and sang, danced, and ate cake
until only the crumbs were left.

When the party was over, Simon's friends began
taking off their party hats, but Simon stopped them.
"Please," he said, "keep the hats on your heads.
Keep the animals in your arms. Take them home with you.
And take the chairs too! I don't want to have MORE, anymore!"

"Thank you! Thank you!" everyone said.
"Oh! What a wonderful party!"

Then Simon the fiddler breathed a sigh of relief.
He had just enough and not too much, and he was perfectly happy
again.